a gift
for the
███████████
████ Library
Media Center
from

████████████
███████████

on his
7th birthday
May 10, 1991

TODDLECREEK POST OFFICE

URI SHULEVITZ

Farrar, Straus and Giroux

New York

To Walter and Henrietta Ulmer
with thanks for telling me about
their days as postmasters

To Harold Leitenberger
master mechanic and friend

The village of Toddlecreek is small. And, like any other small village, it has few houses and few people.

Unlike any other small village, Toddlecreek had its own post office. It was a post office like any other post office. But it was small. Although it was small, the Toddlecreek villagers took pride in it.

Vernon Stamps, the postmaster, was like any other postmaster. Every day, Vernon left his house, and opened his post office the way any other postmaster does. But when Vernon opened his post office, other postmasters were just waking up. When Vernon sorted out the mail, other postmasters were having breakfast. When Vernon had arranged the money orders, registered-mail forms, and stamps on the post-office counter, other postmasters were having their second cup of coffee. By the time other postmasters were bidding their wives good day, Vernon was ready to help customers.

Silken arrived first. Vernon loved dogs, and Silken loved Vernon. She came every day to visit him. She lay down by the door, taking up nearly half the post-office floor. Silken was part wolf and part Alaskan sled dog. She was large, strong, and fierce-looking, but she was very gentle.

The Mayor arrived next. Most mayors are important people. But the Mayor was an old dog. And although everybody knew and liked him, the Mayor had only one place to go to keep warm. So, as on any other day, he came into the post office, sniffed his friends Silken and Vernon, then picked a sunny spot on the floor and lay down.

When tall, skinny Dexter Shuffles shuffled into the post office, Vernon knew it must be nine-thirty. Dexter Shuffles bent his head so as not to scrape it against the top of the doorway, stepped carefully over Silken, and sat down in his spot. Since he lived alone, and had nobody to talk to, Dexter Shuffles sat all day at the post office, telling Vernon about the old horse-and-buggy days on the bumpy Hobblecreek and Stonycrest Roads. Although Vernon knew the stories by heart, he listened to them kindly, as on any other day.

Then Charlie Ax marched in. Charlie Ax had been a logger in lumber camps up north. He nodded to Dexter Shuffles and sat down next to him. And, as on any other day, he waited for his turn to tell Vernon one of his wild stories from his lumber-camp days.

Now Mrs. Woolsox came in with a broken lamp. Some people need their lamp to read books by, others need their lamp to write letters by, but Mrs. Woolsox needed her lamp to knit by, and she asked Vernon to repair it. And Vernon, always ready to help customers, repaired it.

Next came old Abner Flex. It was a chilly day, but old Abner Flex couldn't button his jacket, because it had no buttons. And he couldn't sew any on, because he could barely see. And he couldn't ask his wife to sew them on, because she was long dead. Abner Flex asked Vernon to sew his jacket buttons on. And Vernon, always happy to help customers, sewed them on. Old Abner Flex left the post office, warmer.

When Aurelia Leek and her sons—Tim, Tom, and Todd—came in, the Toddlecreek post office bustled with activity. Aurelia Leek sent a package and bought a money order. She read the bulletin-board announcements to see if there were any barn dances. She pinned up a notice about a couch she wanted to trade for a storm window. She borrowed one of the books that Sally Boone had left the day before. Tim played with the Mayor's tail. Tom played with Silken's ears, and Todd opened her mouth to inspect her sharp teeth. And although the Mayor and Silken would rather nap, they let the boys play as long as they pleased. Then Aurelia Leek left, followed by her sons, Tim, Tom, and Todd.

Every day a band of small dogs assembled near the flower boxes in front of the post office. They didn't go inside, for they knew that although Vernon loved dogs, Silken wouldn't tolerate other dogs inside the post office, except her friend the Mayor.

And it was a day like any other bright spring day. The skies were clear, the sun was shining, birds sang, bees buzzed, and the small dogs barked playfully. Dexter Shuffles went on with his story. Charlie Ax waited for his turn to tell about his lumber-camp days. Silken napped peacefully, while the Mayor enjoyed his sunny spot on the post-office floor. Vernon smiled.

Then clouds dimmed the sun, or so it seemed. Birds' songs diminished, or so it seemed. Bees' buzzing ceased, or so it seemed. The small dogs stopped barking, and stared.

The Toddlecreek post office fell silent. There, standing on the doorstep, was the postal inspector.

The postal inspector surveyed the post office for a very long time. Then she entered and walked slowly around, without saying a word. She stopped to scrutinize the barn-dance announcements, and the notices on the bulletin board. She examined the other books that Sally Boone had left. She looked at Dexter Shuffles and Charlie Ax. Then she glared at Silken and the Mayor.

At long last, she stood before Vernon and said, "A post office is for post-office business only. And it is obvious that a small village like Toddlecreek does not have enough post-office business. Therefore, this post office must be closed."

Dexter Shuffles and Charlie Ax froze. Vernon was stunned. How could he explain that, to the Toddlecreek villagers, their post office was much more than a post office? Vernon could not explain it, so Vernon did not explain it. Vernon said nothing.

And, as on any other day, Vernon carefully stored away the money orders, registered-mail forms, and stamps. But today he also gathered all his belongings. He placed his hammer and screwdriver, needle and thread, pen and pencil, in his briefcase, then put on his coat. And Vernon locked up his post office. And although any other postmaster locks up his post office for the night, Vernon locked up the Toddlecreek post office for the last time.

Vernon left Toddlecreek and went to a post office in a big city far away, where there is much post-office business but little time for a friendly hello.

When weather allowed, Dexter Shuffles shuffled past the deserted post office, daydreaming about the old horse-and-buggy days, and the good times with Vernon at the Toddlecreek post office. And Charlie Ax missed telling Vernon his wild stories from his lumber-camp days. The Mayor was seen wandering around the closed post office. But Silken was never seen again. Some say she went to look for Vernon. Some say she went north to join the wolves. Others say she was killed by a hunter.

Then one day the Toddlecreek post office was torn down. And all that remains are its two flower boxes.

The village of Toddlecreek is small. And, like any other small village, it has few houses and few people. It is not on any map, it is bypassed by travelers and forgotten by time. And, now, like any other small village, Toddlecreek has no post office.